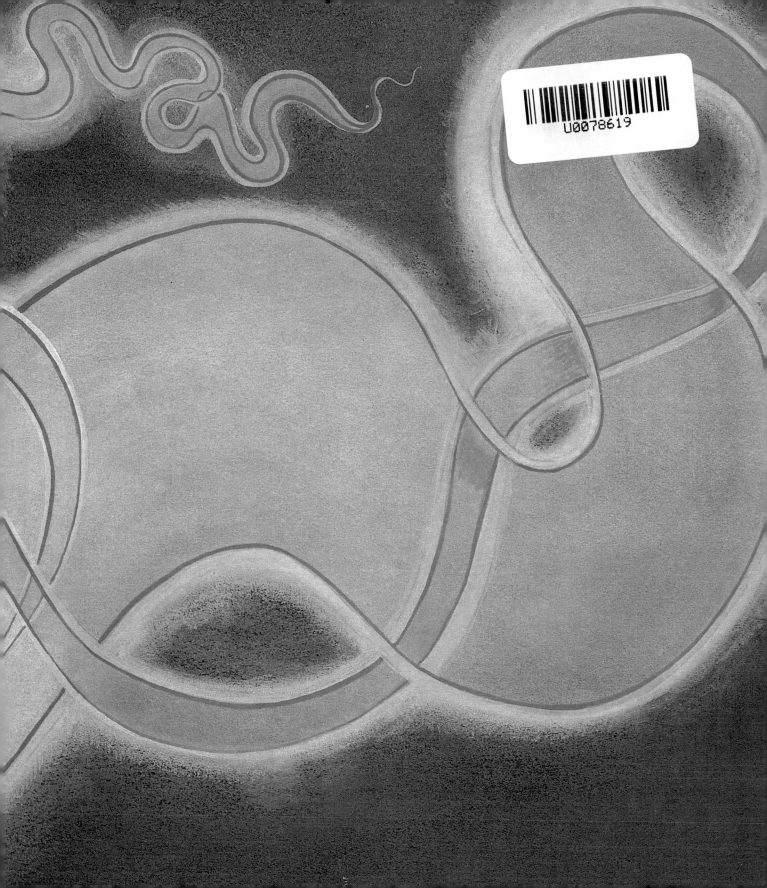

蒙弟闖幽靈屋

Gill Davies 著

Eric Kincaid 繪

洪敦信 譯

三民書局

Haunted House   ISBN 1 85854 775 X

Written by Gill Davies and illustrated by Eric Kincaid

First published in 1998

Under the title Haunted House

by Brimax Books Limited

4/5 Studlands Park Ind. Estate,

Newmarket, Suffolk, CB8 7AU

寂寞小屋
The Lonely House

Monty Mouse likes **exploring**. He loves to **scamper** along finding new places to run and **skip**.

One day when Monty is playing **hide and seek**, he **discovers** an old, **empty** house on the edge of town. It is full of dust and **cobwebs** and seems lonely. Monty says, "You are a nice house. Please can I come in?"

explore [ɪk`splor]
⑩ 探險

scamper [`skæmpɚ]
⑩ 蹦蹦跳跳

skip [skɪp]
⑩ 蹦跳

hide and seek
[`haɪdn̩`sik]
㈎ 捉迷藏

discover [dɪ`skʌvɚ]
⑩ 發現

empty [`ɛmptɪ]
㈡ 空的

cobweb [`kɑb,wɛb]
㈎ 蜘蛛網

小老鼠蒙弟喜歡探險。他最愛蹦蹦跳跳找尋新的地方來奔跑、玩耍。

有一天，蒙弟正在玩捉迷藏時，在鎮郊發現了一棟無人居住的老房子。這個屋子裡佈滿了灰塵和蜘蛛網，好像很寂寞的樣子。

蒙弟說：「你好漂亮喲！我可以進去看看嗎？」

onty calls his brothers and sisters. "Come and look at my lovely **Hideaway** House."
The little mice run everywhere, **peeping** round doors and making the empty house **echo** to the sound of their happy voices. They like the **pantry** best. It is full of food — jars and bottles and cans and bags and **packets**.
"Yum! Yum!" says Sammy. "This place is great!"

hideaway
[`haɪdə,we]
名 藏匿處

peep [pip]
動 老鼠吱吱叫

echo [`ɛko]
動 產生回音

pantry [`pæntrɪ]
名 食物貯藏室

packet [`pækɪt]
名 小包

蒙弟叫來他的兄弟姊妹。「來瞧瞧我那可愛的躲藏小屋吧！」
這群小老鼠在屋子裡又跑又叫，空屋子裡迴盪著他們高興的聲音。他們最喜歡貯藏室了。那裡滿是瓶瓶罐罐和大包小包的食物。
「好耶！好耶！」山咪說。「這地方真棒！」

"**W**hy don't we come and live here?" **suggests** Sammy, **munching** a cookie.

"What a good idea," shouts Monty. "Let's go home and ask." Off **rush** the mice to tell Ma and Pa Whiskers all about the house.

"Hmm," says Pa. "It **certainly sounds interesting**. Your mother and I will take a look tomorrow." And so the next day they all go back to Hideaway House.

suggest [səgˋdʒɛst]
勔 提議

munch [mʌntʃ]
勔 大聲地咀嚼

rush [rʌʃ]
勔 衝

certainly [ˋsɝtn̩lɪ]
副 的確

sound [saʊnd]
勔 聽起來

interesting [ˋɪntərɪstɪŋ]
形 有趣的

「我們為什麼不搬來這兒住呢？」山咪大聲嚼著餅乾，邊提議說。
「好主意吔！」蒙弟大聲說。「我們回家問問吧！」老鼠們便衝回家去告訴老鼠爸爸和媽媽這房子的事。
「嗯！」爸爸說。「這聽起來確實蠻有趣的。我和你們的媽媽明天就去瞧瞧吧！」於是第二天，他們全都去到了那棟躲藏小屋。

Ma and Pa Whiskers think Hideaway House is **wonderful**. "We will **move** here right away," they say. "Let us go home and **pack**."

So the very next day the Whisker family put all their **belongings** into Pa's **matchstick cart** and move into their new house.

As soon as they **arrive**, Monty Mouse goes upstairs to explore.

wonderful
[`wʌndə-fəl]
形 美妙的

move [muv]
動 移動

pack [pæk]
動 包裝

belongings
[bə`lɔŋɪŋz]
名 所有物

matchstick
[`mætʃ,stɪk]
名 火柴棒

cart [kart]
名 手推車

arrive [ə`raɪv]
動 到達

老鼠爸爸和媽媽覺得這棟躲藏小屋棒極了。「我們立刻就搬來這兒。」他們說。「我們回家打包吧！」

就這樣，隔天老鼠一家子就把所有的家當放進爸爸的火柴盒推車，搬進了他們的新家。

他們一到達那兒，小老鼠蒙弟便上樓探險去了。

This is what Monty likes best. He runs everywhere, **sniffing** out every **corner** from the cool, dark cellar to the hot, dusty **attic**. Then he explores all the **secret** places in the **tangled**, **overgrown** garden. Monty is very happy. And so is Hideaway House. It is no longer sad and lonely. In fact, it is the happiest house in town.

sniff [snɪf]
動 嗅

corner [ˋkɔrnɚ]
名 角落

attic [ˋætɪk]
名 閣樓

secret [ˋsikrɪt]
形 隱蔽的

tangle [ˋtæŋgl̩]
動 糾結

overgrown
[ˋovɚˋgron]
形 叢生的

蒙弟最喜歡探險了。他到處跑來跑去，從冰冷、陰暗的地下室到悶熱、滿是灰塵的小閣樓，他嗅遍了每一個角落。然後，他來到雜草叢生的花園，想找出花園裡所有隱蔽的地方。

蒙弟非常快樂呢！這棟躲藏小屋也很快樂喲！它不再悲傷和寂寞了。事實上，它現在可是鎮上最快樂的屋子了！

蒙弟撞見幽靈

Monty Mouse Meets Ghost

"I like night time in the garden," says Monty as he runs outside to **smell** the **honeysuckle** one warm summer night.

Far away the town lights **gleam** and **sparkle**.
"Be **careful** that the owls don't eat you," calls Ma, but Monty is not afraid. He is friends with the owls, the bats, and the **beetles**.

smell [smɛl]
勔 嗅

honeysuckle [ˋhʌnɪ͵sʌkl̩]
名 金銀花

gleam [glim]
勔 閃爍

sparkle [ˋspɑrkl̩]
勔 閃耀

careful [ˋkɛrfəl]
形 小心的

beetle [ˋbitl̩]
名 金龜子

在一個溫暖的夏夜，蒙弟邊跑出去聞金銀花的香味，邊說：「我喜歡晚上待在花園裡。」遠處鎮上的燈火一閃一閃地發出光亮。

「小心啊！可不要被貓頭鷹吃了！」媽媽喊著。蒙弟可不害怕呢！貓頭鷹、蝙蝠和金龜子全是他的朋友。

onty scampers a little way along the path, and then suddenly he sees a **ghost**!

A **wavy**, white shape rises out of the **undergrowth** as Monty **rubs** his eyes in **amazement**.

"Wooooooooo!" says the shape.

"Ooooooooeeer!" says Monty.

"Wooooooooo!" says the shape again, moving up the path and coming closer to Monty.

ghost [gost]
名 幽靈，鬼

wavy [ˋwevɪ]
形 波浪狀的

undergrowth [ˋʌndəˏgroθ]
名 草叢

rub [rʌb]
動 揉

amazement [əˋmezmənt]
名 驚訝

蒙弟沿著小徑蹦蹦跳跳了一小段路，突然間，他看見一個幽靈。
一個波浪狀的白色幽靈從草叢中升起，蒙弟吃驚地揉著眼睛。
「嗚……！」那個幽靈發出聲來。
「啊……！」蒙弟叫了起來。
「嗚……！」幽靈又發出聲音，還移動到小路上，逐漸向蒙弟靠了過來。

17

"oooooeeer!" says Monty again, walking rapidly **backward**.
"I am the Ghost of Hideaway House," **announces** the shape, **pulling** himself **up** tall. "Wooooo!"
Monty stares up in **astonishment**.
"Wooo," **wails** Ghost again. "Why aren't you running away?"
"There is nowhere left to run," answers Monty, his back **pressed** against the wall.

backward [`bækwə·d]
副 向後地

announce [ə`naʊns]
動 宣佈

pull up
拉起

astonishment
[ə`stɑnɪʃmənt]
名 驚嚇

wail [wel]
動 哀嚎

press [prɛs]
動 壓

「啊……！」蒙弟又叫了起來，快速地後退。
「我就是那棟躲藏小屋裡的幽靈，」幽靈挺直了身子說。「嗚……！」
蒙弟嚇得瞪大了眼睛。
「嗚……」幽靈又哀嚎了起來。「你為什麼不跑了呢？」
「我已經沒有地方可逃了。」蒙弟背部緊緊抵著牆壁說。

"Anyway," says Monty, **upset** that his evening walk is being **spoiled**, "you should be **haunting** the house not the garden." And then suddenly Ghost **sinks** down and begins to cry.
"I know," he **sobs**, "but the house is full of animals now. There's an owl in the haunted bedroom, and there's no room left for me."

upset [ʌpˋsɛt]
形 憤怒的

spoil [spɔɪl]
動 破壞

haunt [hɔnt]
動 （幽靈）出沒

sink [sɪŋk]
動 沮喪

sob [sɑb]
動 啜泣

「不管怎麼樣，」蒙弟很不高興他的夜間散步被破壞了，他說：「你該在屋子裡出現，而不是花園呀！」
幽靈一下子變得很沮喪，還哭了起來。
「我知道啊！」他啜泣著說，「可是房子裡現在滿滿的全是動物。在我常去的臥室裡，就有一隻貓頭鷹，根本沒有剩下的房間給我嘛！」

21

Tears **roll** down Ghost's face.

"I think," says Monty, "that you had better come inside."

"You **poor** dear!" says Ma, seeing Ghost's sad face. "You look as if you need some nice apple **pie** to **cheer** you **up**."

Ghost smiles through his tears. "I haven't eaten apple pie for a long, long time — not once since I have been dead," he says.

tear [tɪr]
名 眼淚

roll [rol]
動 滾落

poor [pʊr]
形 可憐的

pie [paɪ]
名 派

cheer up
振作

眼淚滾落幽靈的臉龐。
「我想，」蒙弟說，「你還是進來屋子裡比較好！」
「你好可憐喲！」媽媽看著幽靈悲傷的面容說。「看來你好像需要一些可口的蘋果派來振作振作！」
幽靈破涕為笑。「我已經好久、好久沒吃過蘋果派了——從我死了以後就沒吃過了。」他說。

Ghost eats three fat **slices** of pie. It is **delicious** and he feels much better. Then Monty takes Ghost upstairs and shows him the **spare** bedroom on the top floor.
"This can be yours," he says.
Now Ghost is very happy. He has a lovely room with a **view** over the railway line, lots of new friends, and lots of apple pie.

slice [slaɪs]
名 片

delicious [dɪˋlɪʃəs]
形 美味的

spare [spɛr]
形 剩下的

view [vju]
名 風景

幽靈一連吃下三大片的蘋果派。蘋果派的美味使他覺得好多了。接著蒙弟帶他上樓，給他看頂樓剩下的臥室。
「這個房間就是你的了。」他說。
幽靈現在非常快樂。他擁有一個看得到鐵路風景的好房間，有了許多的新朋友，還有很多很多的蘋果派呢！

中英對照，既可學英語又可了解偉人小故事哦！

超級科學家系列
SUPER SCIENTISTS

當彗星掠過哈雷眼前，
當蘋果落在牛頓頭頂，
當電燈泡在愛迪生手中亮起……
一個個求知的心靈與真理所碰撞出的火花，
就是《超級科學家系列》！

神祕元素：居禮夫人的故事
電燈的發明：愛迪生的故事
望遠天際：伽利略的故事
光的顏色：牛頓的故事
爆炸性的發現：諾貝爾的故事
蠶寶寶的祕密：巴斯德的故事
宇宙教授：愛因斯坦的故事
命運的彗星：哈雷的故事

寂寞小屋
蒙弟撞見幽靈

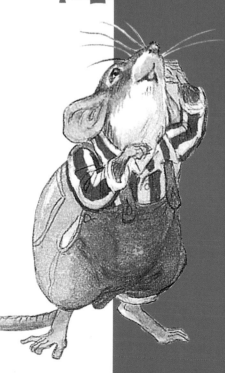

網際網路位址　http：// www. sanmin. com. tw

ⓒ 寂寞小屋／蒙弟撞見幽靈

著作人　Gill Davies
繪圖者　Eric Kincaid
譯　者　洪敦信
發行人　劉振強
著作財　三民書局股份有限公司
產權人
　　　　臺北市復興北路三八六號
發行所　三民書局股份有限公司
　　　　地址／臺北市復興北路三八六號
　　　　電話／二五○○六六○○
　　　　郵撥／○○○九九九八——五號
印刷所　三民書局股份有限公司
門市部　復北店／臺北市復興北路三八六號
　　　　重南店／臺北市重慶南路一段六十一號
初　版　中華民國八十八年十一月
編　號　S85516
定　價　新臺幣壹佰伍拾元整
行政院新聞局登記證局版臺業字第○二○○號

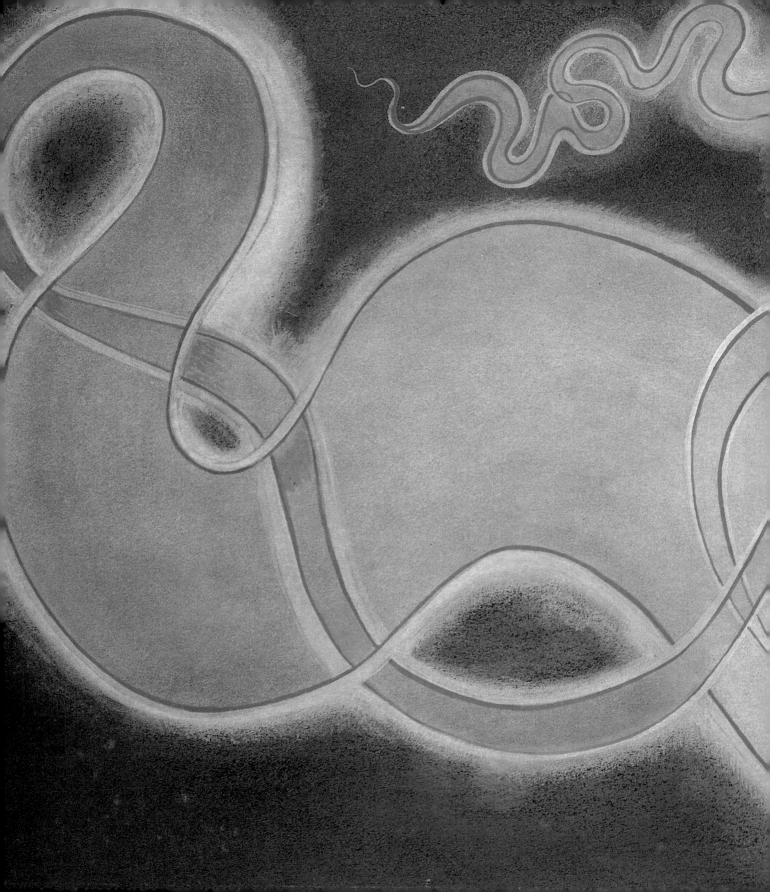